THE LITTLE SNOWPLOW WISHES FOR SNOW

LORA KOEHLER   illustrated by JAKE PARKER

CANDLEWICK PRESS

The little snowplow loved his job on the Mighty Mountain Road Crew.
All year long, he helped the other trucks with their digging, pulling, and lifting.

But the little snowplow loved plowing snow best of all,
so he always wished for a snowy winter.

In spring, he searched until he found a four-leaf clover
to wish on.

In summer, his wish sailed on the breeze
with the dandelion seeds.

When fall arrived, he stayed up late
to wish on a shooting star.

Finally, cold winds started to blow.
Time for snow!

The little snowplow went through his exercises to make
sure everything was in working order.

Beep, beep!

Then he tuned in to the weather forecast.

No snow.

He drove to the top of the mountain.
Gray clouds stacked high into the sky.

But no snow.

"What we need is a way to welcome winter," the cement mixer said.
"How about the snowkey-pokey—on ice?" suggested the water truck.

All the trucks honked and beeped and blinked.
The water truck sprayed the back parking lot.

The moon rose. The water froze.

In the morning, trucks slipped and slid onto the ice.
They put their bumpers in, they took their bumpers
out, they put their bumpers in, and they shook them
all about.

There were only a few mishaps.

When the little snowplow got back to the garage, he felt happy—and hopeful. The first day of winter was only days away. Surely it would snow then.

But the winter solstice brought glittering stars, not snow.
The little snowplow carried firewood to the park for a
bonfire to light up the longest night of the year.

January brought northern lights, but no snow. The little snowplow graded trails.

February brought flurries, but nothing stuck. The little snowplow delivered valentines.

The little snowplow's birthday was at the beginning of March, and as it drew closer, he started to worry.

"I heard this is the warmest winter ever!" the cement mixer said. "Don't listen to her," said the steamroller. "I'm sure we'll have snow soon."

"Or maybe we'll go the whole winter without any snow at all," the dump truck said.

The little snowplow turned his bumper on THAT horrible thought. He focused instead on planning his birthday party.

First he invited his friends.

Then he made snow decorations and planned snow games.

At least we can pretend we have snow, the little snowplow thought.

But when he woke up the morning of his birthday . . .

SNOW!

His birthday party would have to wait.
He had a job to do!

Beep, beep, VROOOM!

The little snowplow plowed the streets of Mighty Mountain.

But it kept snowing.

So he plowed the streets again.

But it still kept snowing.

His headlights started to sag. His plow started to drag.

He wondered if the other trucks were celebrating his birthday
without him.

As he plowed Silver Fork, he heard a rumbling.

MAIN ST

SILVER FORK

He turned onto Main Street.

"Surprise! All clear!" His friends honked and beeped and blinked.

"*HAPPY BIRTHDAY!*"

Together they paraded back to the garage.

They played pin the tail on the yeti.

They made snow trucks.

They had a snow battle.

Then the dump truck brought out a cake.

When the little snowplow blew out the
candles, he made a wish . . .

for more snow.

Beep, beep, VROOOM!

For Devin and Cade. Let it snow!

L. K.

To Don and Laurie

J. P.

First edition 2019

Library of Congress Catalog Card Number pending
ISBN 978-1-5362-0117-8

19 20 21 22 23 24 CCP 10 9 8 7 6 5 4 3 2 1

Printed in Shenzhen, Guangdong, China

This book was typeset in PMN Caecilia.
The illustrations were done in pencil and rendered digitally.

Candlewick Press
99 Dover Street
Somerville, Massachusetts 02144

visit us at www.candlewick.com